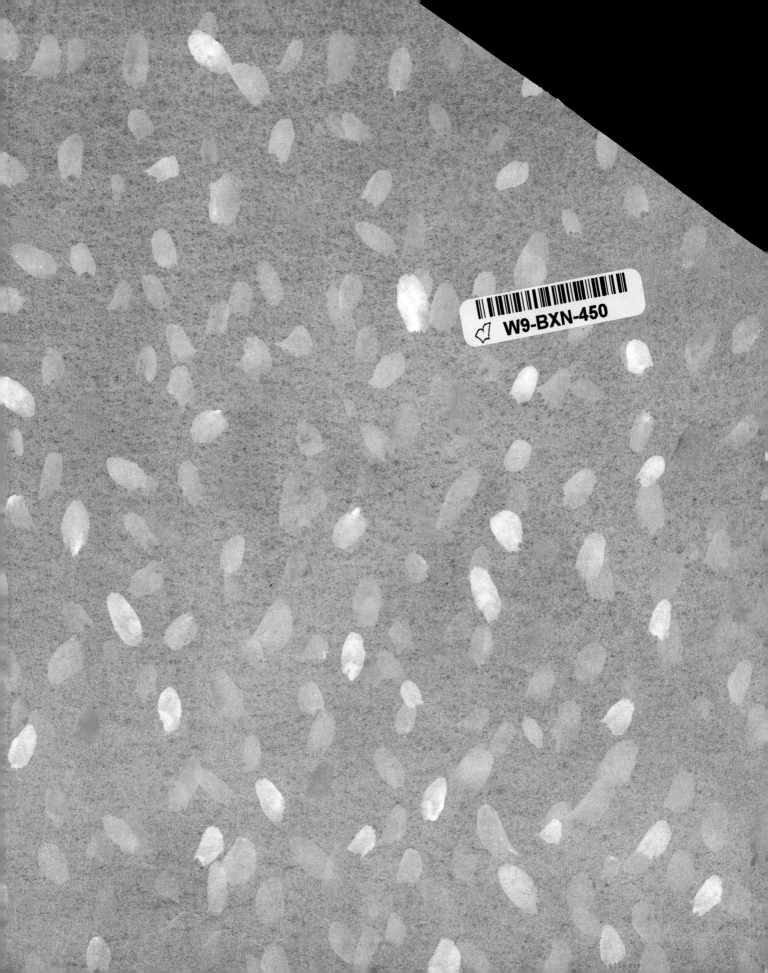

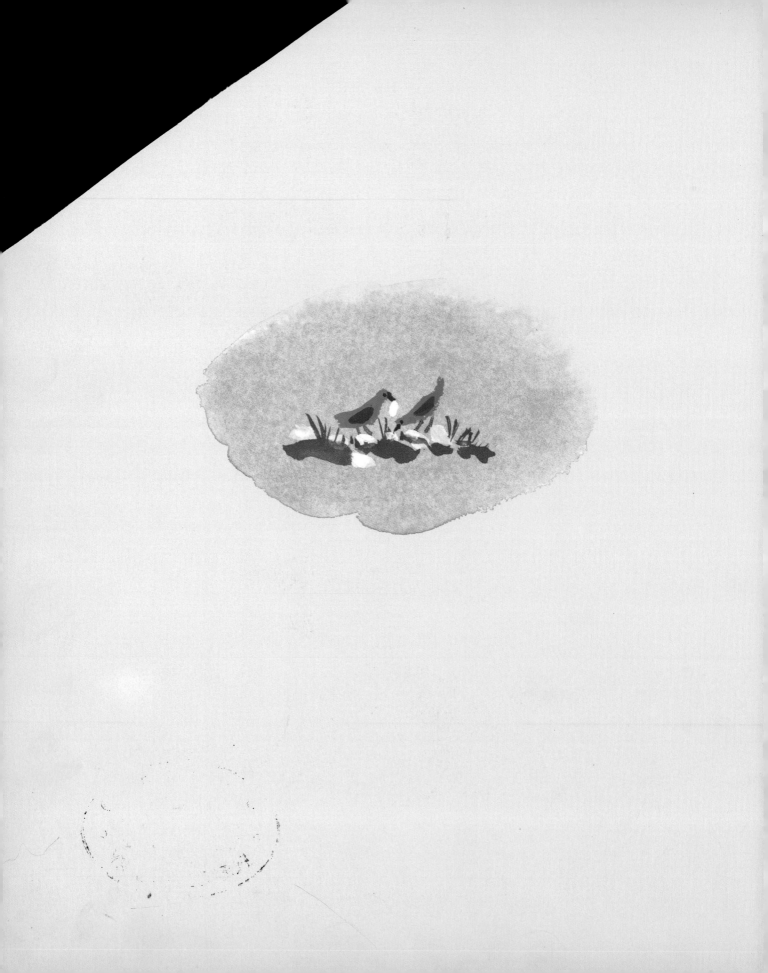

Fletcher
and the
Springtime
Blossoms

BY JULIA RAWLINSON
PICTURES BY TIPHANIE BEEKE

GREENWILLOW BOOKS, AN IMPRINT OF HarperCollinsPublishers

The woods were full of the chirping, bustling, singsong sounds of spring. Fletcher bounced along with his nose in the air, sniffing the just-burst buds of flowers and playing chase with butterflies. With his head spinning with sights and sounds . . .

he tumbled happily down the hill into the sunny orchard. But when he picked himself up from the ground, he couldn't believe his eyes.

A soft breeze danced through the branches, carrying snowy flakes. Snow so late in spring, thought Fletcher. It will be too cold for the buds and butterflies. There's no time to lose.

Looking for someone to tell,
he trotted back up the hill and passed
a pair of birds coo-cooing on a branch.

"You've flown to your summer home too soon," Fletcher cried.
"I've been down to the orchard, and there's more snow on the way."
"Then we should fly back south," they called. "But first we must
tell Porcupine. He's just come out of his bed of leaves. He needs
to snuggle back down, or he'll freeze."

Fletcher and the birds found Porcupine stretching and scritch-scratching.

"There's snow on the way," panted Fletcher. "I saw it in the orchard. It will be too cold for the butterflies, the birds will need to fly south, and you must hide away."

"Then I should crawl back into my bed," snuffled Porcupine, sadly. "But first we must tell Squirrel that he needs to hunt for food. He's eaten his winter store of nuts. He'll need to find some more."

Fletcher, the birds, and Porcupine found Squirrel scampering
after sunbeams.
"Snow is blowing in from the orchard," gasped Fletcher.
"It will be too cold for the butterflies, the birds will need
to fly south, poor Porcupine must go back to bed, and
you must find some food."
"You're right. I've eaten my spring feast," said Squirrel,
"and all my stores are gone. But before I hunt for more,
we need to tell the rabbits to munch as much grass as
they can before the snow falls."

Fletcher, the birds, Porcupine, and Squirrel hurried off again.

The rabbits were rolling down the hill next to their burrow.
"Stop playing!" cried Fletcher. "There's snow blowing in from
the orchard. It will be too cold for the butterflies, the birds
will need to fly south, poor Porcupine must go back to bed,
Squirrel needs to find food, and you must munch more grass."

"Before we eat," said the rabbits, staggering dizzily to their feet . . .

"Let's go and play in the snow!"

So the rabbits hoppity-roly-poly-plopped down the hill, through the woods.

They were chased by Squirrel, Porcupine, the birds, and a bouncy, full-of-importance fox, all the way to the orchard, where the ground was white with . . . .

BLOSSOMS!

Blossoms bobbing in the branches. Blossoms blowing in the breeze.
Blossoms blanketing the ground, and not a snowflake to be found.

"Those are blossoms, not snow, you foolish fox!" the animals cried.
Fletcher blinked and rubbed his eyes, feeling very silly. But then . . .

the animals scooped up pawfuls and clawfuls of blossoms
from the ground, and covered him in a tickly shower
of fluttering white petals! Fletcher and his friends
ran and played between the trees, until at
last they all collapsed in a blossomy,
soft white heap.

Then the birds fluttered
back to their branch with
beakfuls of blossoms to
line their nest.

Porcupine snuffled off
up the slope, his quills
dotted with tiny white
petals.

Squirrel went chasing up and down trees after snow-white petals dancing in the breeze,

and the rabbits bounced back up the hill with blossoms to brighten their burrow.

But Fletcher just lay smiling in his soft bed of petals,
watching the blossoming branches bobbing overhead.

For Ben and Tom, with love and thanks—J. R.

For Sarah, Thea, and Silas, who love the snow—T. B.

Fletcher and the Springtime Blossoms, Text copyright © 2009 by Julia Rawlinson

Illustrations copyright © 2009 by Tiphanie Beeke

All rights reserved. Manufactured in China.

www.harpercollinschildrens.com

Pastels were used to prepare the full-color art. The text type is Glouces Old Style.

Library of Congress Cataloging-in-Publication Data

Rawlinson, Julia.

Fletcher and the springtime blossoms / by Julia Rawlinson ; illustrated by Tiphanie Beeke.

p. cm.

"Greenwillow Books." Summary: When Fletcher the fox finds the ground covered in white, he rushes to warn the other animals that spring snow has fallen, but when they follow him back to the meadow they find something much more fun.

ISBN 978-0-06-168855-3 (trade bdg.)

[1. Foxes—Fiction. 2. Forest animals—Fiction. 3. Flowers—Fiction. 4. Spring—Fiction.]

I. Beeke, Tiphanie, ill. II. Title.

PZ7.R1974Flh 2009 [E]—dc22 2008012643

First Edition 10 9 8 7 6 5 4 3 2 1

Greenwillow Books

JJ
Rawlinson
Julia